PUFFIN BOOKS

# THE RAILWAY CAT'S SECRET

It's a hard life being a railway cat when no one wants you around. Poor Alfie doesn't know what on earth is going on at the station and no one will tell him – all he *does* know is that he seems to be in the way. Then he discovers a thrilling secret of his very own – and he's determined to *keep* it a secret!

Phyllis Arkle was born and educated in Chester, but now lives in Berkshire. She has written about Alfie and his friends in two other Young Puffins: *The Railway Cat* and *The Railway Cat and Digby*.

*Other books by Phyllis Arkle*

Magic at Midnight
Magic in the Air
The Railway Cat
The Railway Cat and Digby
The Village Dinosaur
Two Village Dinosaurs

PHYLLIS ARKLE

# The
# Railway Cat's
# Secret

*Illustrated by Lynne Byrnes*

## PUFFIN BOOKS

Puffin Books, Penguin Books Ltd, Harmondsworth, Middlesex, England
Viking Penguin Inc., 40 West 23rd Street, New York, New York 10010, U.S.A.
Penguin Books Australia Ltd, Ringwood, Victoria, Australia
Penguin Books Canada Ltd, 2801 John Street, Markham, Ontario, Canada L3R 1B4
Penguin Books (N.Z.) Ltd, 182–190 Wairau Road, Auckland 10, New Zealand

First published by Hodder & Stoughton Ltd 1985
Published in Puffin Books 1987

Made and printed in Great Britain by
Richard Clay Ltd, Bungay, Suffolk
Typeset in Plantin

# Contents

# 1

# Station Cleaning

Alfie, the railway cat, was disgusted – station cleaning time *again*? And what a cleaning! The staff seemed to have gone berserk. They bustled about as though there wasn't a minute to lose.

Between trains they swept, scrubbed, polished all the furniture and fittings and weeded the flower beds. Passengers alighting from trains were hurried out of the station, while others joining trains were ushered on board without ceremony. All very undignified, thought Alfie, puzzled.

Even Alfie's special friend, Chargeman Fred, had no time for the railway cat. 'Not now, Alfie,' he said firmly, but kindly, as Alfie, miaowing loudly, weaved in and out of the man's legs.

And, 'Clear off, Alfie!' yelled Leading Railman Hack as he tripped and caught his ankle a sharp blow with a broom. (Not my fault this time, thought Alfie!)

But, 'Ouch! Ow . . . don't want to see any more of *you* today,' screamed Hack.

'Brr . . . brr . . . brr . . .' growled Alfie. He never expected any sympathy from Hack.

Brown, the booking clerk, popped his head round the office door. 'Phew – such a commotion!' he cried. 'What's it all in aid of?'

'Wish I knew,' said Hack.

'Miaow!' said Alfie. So do I.

Alfie sat down and watched Fred as he darted about the station, giving orders, changing his mind and then charging off somewhere else. It was so unlike his friend to go about tight-lipped, with a frown on his forehead and an air of secrecy about him.

Something clicked in Alfie's mind. Secrecy? That was it. Fred must have a *secret* which he wasn't allowed to tell anyone about – not even the railway cat! Poor Fred. No wonder he looked worried.

Fred came towards him. 'Ah, there you are,

Alfie,' he cried (apparently forgetting he had just been ignoring the railway cat). 'I think I'll start on you next.'

Start on me, thought Alfie? That meant only one thing – a good clean. He wasn't going to put up with that if he could help it. He was quite capable of looking after himself, thank you.

So he turned swiftly and, with tail down, set off at a good pace down the platform. Fred followed. 'Come here, Alfie. *Come here*,' he shouted, as he waved his arms.

But leaving the station behind him, Alfie started running along the top of the embankment. He could hear Fred calling, 'Come back, Alfie. Come b . . a . . . c . . . . k . . . .'

Alfie slowed down when Fred was out of earshot, but he went on and on, much further than he had ventured for a long time. Eventually he came to a small wayside station, which had been closed for over a year.

Weeds grew out of cracks on the platform and a rusty gate in a broken-down fence hung askew. Alfie paused to gaze at a small building, once a waiting room and booking office combined. He jumped up on to a sill and looked through a slit in the boarded-up window. Light filtered in from a broken rear window and he could see an old table and a rickety chair.

Wandering round to the back of the station Alfie found what was once a tidy garden, a tangled mass of bushes and weeds. He glanced round in dismay. What a pity. Then he thought – but what a lovely stalking place.

On his stomach he slowly wormed his way through the undergrowth keeping his eyes and ears open all the time. He had gone a short distance when, to his surprise, he emerged into a real garden. A vegetable plot with neat rows of onions, carrots, cabbages and lettuce, and stakes for peas and beans – quite hidden from view, a secret garden! There was no one in sight.

Who was the gardener? Why was it a *secret* garden? Alfie felt quite excited as he always enjoyed a mystery. He decided to wait and see if anyone turned up. He lay down between two rows of vegetables, but soon became drowsy

10

and fell asleep. After a time he woke up, yawned and stretched himself as he looked round. Still no one about. Very odd.

He left the little station and continued his walk along the embankment. Coming to a tunnel he peered through the opening and saw light streaming in from the other end. When he heard a couple of hoots in the distance he drew back and sat down in the long grass. Soon – with a whoosh! and a roar! – a freight train entered the tunnel, and hooted again as it passed Alfie.

He watched the train until it was out of sight, then he stretched himself lazily and flopped down on his side. He thought about Fred. Was it really necessary for his friend to be so secretive? Why didn't he tell the railway cat about it?

After a time Alfie got to his feet, stretched again and yawned, before deciding he'd better return and see if Fred had calmed down. In any case he was feeling hungry.

So Alfie set off home. As he approached the wayside station he spied a rabbit scampering along the platform. Alfie chased it to the back of the station, and then right through the bushes.

As he emerged into the secret garden Alfie halted to take a quick look round, and lost sight of the rabbit – but no matter, thought Alfie. There was no sign of life in the garden and no sound except for a slight breeze rustling the leaves. It was very eerie, thought Alfie, as he turned and ran all the way back to his own station.

Fred was still busy. So was Hack and everyone else. They ignored Alfie. He tried rubbing a cheek against Fred's leg. Then he stretched up and clawed at his friend's jacket. 'Miaow! Miaow!' he cried. Can't we have a bit of fun?

'*Now* what's the matter, Alfie?' sighed Fred.

'Not getting enough attention, that's what's the matter with him,' put in Hack, scornfully.

'Brr . . . rr . . . rr . . .' howled Alfie.

'Swearing at me again!' cried Hack.

'Don't be ridiculous, Hack!' shouted Fred. 'Feed Alfie and lock him up or we'll never get on.'

Alfie was furious. How could Fred let him down like this? He made a dash down the platform, but Hack lunged forward and grabbed him in a rugby-like tackle.

'Miaow! Miaow! Mi . . ao . . . w . . . .' screeched Alfie as he turned his head and bit Hack's little finger.

'Aargh . . . aargh!' cried Hack as he shook his hand. His grip tightened as Alfie struggled to free himself. Fred came running.

'He bit me!' shouted Hack. 'I'll teach him his manners. I'll train him to . . .'

'Oh, for goodness sake, stop blathering, Hack!' cried Fred. 'Here, give him to me.'

Fred snatched Alfie and carried him into the staff room. He put two bowls on the floor, filled one with raw meat and vegetables and the other with milk. Then he went out, slammed the door behind him, and turned the key in the lock.

And all without a word or a miaow uttered. Alfie couldn't believe it. He was so upset that he ate only half the meat but managed to finish the milk. He spent a very uneasy night and woke

15

long before his usual time. There was a lot more noise than usual when the staff came on duty.

Whatever was going on now? wondered Alfie. No one came to see him, so he howled and howled. When that had no effect he jumped up and rattled the door handle. He did this dozens of times before he heard a key in the lock.

Fred appeared. He shook his head at Alfie. 'Really, Alfie,' he said. 'Here am I trying to get the station ship-shape for what I hope will be a very happy occasion, while you're making all this fuss and bother.'

'Miaow!' cried Alfie. You're making a lot of fuss and bother yourself.

'If you ask me . . .' began Fred.

'Miaow!' put in Alfie. I didn't.

'. . . I'm fed up with trying to keep a secret,' said Fred, as he banged the table with his fist.

'Miaow!' said Alfie yet again. Surely you could tell me?

'It's like this, Alfie,' Fred went on. 'I've had definite instructions from Headquarters to keep the matter a close secret, as they . . . er . . . er

. . . the party concerned, that is, want to spend a nice peaceful time here at the station – incognito, if you get my meaning.'

Alfie didn't understand the last bit, but who was the party concerned? he wondered. Could it be the Lord Mayor? Or the Chancellor of the Exchequer? Or a Pop Group? A Pop Group would be fine. Even Hack would enjoy that.

'Just be seen and not heard today, Alfie,' said Fred. 'To please me.'

Alfie followed him on to the platform, where he stopped short in horror. All was confusion. The *painters* had moved in. Ladders were propped against walls, and doors were being rubbed down before being painted. Alfie shuddered at the thought of paint getting on to his fur and of people ordering him out of the way. There would be no peace.

Fred grew more and more annoyed, as miaowing all the time, Alfie followed him everywhere, up and down platforms, over the bridge and back again and into the office. Whenever Fred stopped Alfie jumped up at him, wanting to play if only for a few minutes.

But Fred refused. 'Alfie, this is just too much,' he raged at last. 'If you can't behave in a sensible manner, I'll have to send you away for a day or two, and you'll miss all the excitement.'

'Miaow!' hissed Alfie. All work and no play was making Fred bad-tempered, but it would take a sledgehammer to knock sense into his friend's brains just now. Alfie looked behind him at the chaos on the station as, once again, he set off briskly along the top of the embankment – to get away from it all for a time.

He didn't pause at the wayside station. When he came to the tunnel he ran down the embankment and cautiously glanced inside to look again at the circle of light at the far end.

Suddenly, he heard a faint noise inside the tunnel – a bird, perhaps? He listened. All was quiet for a time, then the sound was heard again, very softly, 'Miaow!' Alfie stiffened in dismay. There must be a *cat* inside the tunnel. How dangerous!

What could he do?

18

## 2

# The Rescue

Alfie hesitated, then, with a quick glance up and down the lines, he rushed into the tunnel – something he had never done before. It was very gloomy inside, but he could just see stones strewn along the track and he noticed an empty cigarette packet and half a tomato near a shiny rail.

Another faint miaow guided him to a tiny ginger kitten lying in the middle of the fast track. Bending his head Alfie could see that her right foreleg was bent in an unnatural position beneath her body, while her left foreleg was almost touching the rail. The kitten tried to rise but fell back helplessly.

Alfie licked the kitten's shoulder before running back through the tunnel. Instinctively he headed for his own station, but at the little wayside station he stopped, turned, and darted

round to the back. He pushed his way through the undergrowth. As he came to the edge of the secret garden he heard someone coughing, 'Hhrraaagh!' He peeped out and saw a man digging.

The man's shirt was torn and his trousers were hitched up round his knees with string. Must be a tramp, thought Alfie. He miaowed softly. As the tramp turned round Alfie saw that he had a kind, sun-tanned face. However, not observing the railway cat in the bushes, the man shrugged his shoulders and resumed digging.

Alfie crept from under cover. Taking the man by surprise, he wailed loudly, 'M . . I . . . A . . . . O . . . . . W . . . . . .!'

The tramp jumped, dropped his spade and turned round again. 'Why, hello, old chap!' he cried. 'You did give me a fright. Where have you sprung from?' He bent down and stroked Alfie.

Alfie stretched up and pulled hard at the man's trousers with his claws. Then he ran off. After a few yards he stopped and looked round hopefully. 'Miaow!' he cried. Oh, for goodness sake – *come on*!

But the man laughed. 'Sorry,' he said, 'I'm far too busy to play games.'

Alfie rushed back, jumped up nearly pushing the man over before running off again and then stopping. His tail went flick, flick, flick all the time as he waited.

Mystified, the tramp gazed at Alfie. 'Hmmm,' he murmured. 'Wonder what you want? Is something worrying you?'

'Miaow!' cried Alfie. Of course there is!

The man hesitated before deciding to follow Alfie through the bushes and to the tunnel entrance. Alfie set off into the tunnel, but the man shouted, 'Come back. It's not safe in there!'

Alfie returned reluctantly, looked up at the man and said, 'Miaow!' Please understand.

There was silence and then came a faint miaow which echoed eerily in the tunnel. 'My word!' exclaimed the tramp. 'There's a cat in there.' He glanced at his wrist watch. 'Only five or six minutes before the next train is due – just enough time for me to run back for a torch. You wait here.' Alfie watched the man scramble up the embankment and race off towards the secret garden. He returned in a matter of minutes and dashed past Alfie on his way to the kitten.

Alfie waited, his eyes and ears on the alert all the time for the approach of the next train. Would the tramp find the kitten? Would he get her out safely? It seemed a very long time before the man, with the kitten cradled in his arms, stumbled out of the tunnel just as a couple of hoots were heard. He knelt down behind a bush until a train had passed at speed.

'Phew! That was a narrow shave!' he gasped as he got up and wiped his forehead with the back of a hand.

'Miaow!' cried Alfie. Well done!

The kitten miaowed mournfully and closed her eyes. 'Come on,' said the man with a jerk of his head towards the little station. 'Urgent first aid is required.'

He led the way back and entered the waiting

room through the rear door. Alfie followed. The man closed the door before gently laying the kitten on her side on the table. Alfie leapt lightly on to the chair to ensure having a good view of the proceedings.

With the utmost care the tramp ran his hands over the kitten's limbs. Once when the kitten jerked in pain he stroked her reassuringly. 'All right. All right,' he said. 'I'll soon put you right.' He turned to Alfie. 'Foreleg fractured in two places,' he said briefly. 'I'll need the first aid box from my secret hiding place in the garden. You stay and keep her company.'

Alfie didn't move an inch until the tramp returned with an armful of articles which he placed on the table. First he filled a saucer with milk from a bottle. 'A drink first!' he cried as he held the saucer in front of the kitten's mouth. Alfie watched eagerly as she feebly put out a pink tongue and managed to lap a little milk.

'She'll be fine soon,' said the man as he opened the small first aid box. Alfie leaned forward, put one paw on the table, and

anxiously watched the man's movements.

'Don't worry!' said the man as he gave Alfie a playful push back on to the chair. 'I know what I'm doing – I hold a first aid certificate.'

'Miaow!' said Alfie, relieved to hear that.

'My name's Joe,' the man told Alfie as he started to examine the injured limb. 'I'm down on my luck as I've been out of work for months.' He sighed. 'Trouble is I'm an independent sort of chap – don't want to go on the dole. Rather earn my own living.'

Joe stopped talking as he gave all his attention to the job in hand. Alfie watched intently. Once Joe stretched up and put a hand to his back. 'Ouch!' he cried. 'Wrenched my back pushing too heavy a barrow-load of vegetables. But mustn't grumble. I've been in luck finding this place. I have no right to be here really, so no one – no one, you understand – must find out. It's a secret.'

'Miaow!' said Alfie. You can trust me. Now *I've* got a secret as well as Fred.

Joe went on talking as he dealt with the

kitten. 'I'm making just enough money to keep me going, by selling fruit and vegetables in surrounding villages. Haven't got a car but my barrow comes in useful. Wouldn't do to stop a train and ask for a lift, would it?' He laughed.

Alfie rubbed his chin up and down against the table edge to show his appreciation of the joke.

Joe reached for a plaster. 'You know,' he said, 'it's really doing me good to have someone to talk to. It's very lonely here.'

'Miaow!' said Alfie. I'm ready to listen any time.

'Normally I only use this room at night when there's little chance of being found out.' He tapped the table and pointed at the chair. 'An old table, a chair and a camp-bed which I bring in at night make a home for me.'

Joe was silent for a time as he carefully bound up the patient's leg. When he had finished he stood back and gazed at the kitten. 'There now – finished!' he said triumphantly. 'She'll be quite all right in a week or two. Meanwhile I'll have to hide her in the garden during the day, but she can come in here with me at night. But heaven knows what I'm going to give her to eat!' He rubbed the soft fur under the kitten's chin. 'Listen!' cried Joe. 'I can hear her purring.'

'Miaow!' cried Alfie, delighted. So can I.

'Wonder what her name is?' mused Joe. 'I think I'll call her Tansy – a herb I've been planting in the garden this morning. What do you think?'

'Miaow!' agreed Alfie. It suits her.

'Back to gardening,' said Joe. 'There's an extra mouth to feed now, so I'll have to work harder to earn more money.' He picked up Tansy and went outside. Alfie jumped off the chair and followed. 'What about you – have you got some business to attend to?'

'Miaow!' replied Alfie. Yes. Time I went to see how Fred's getting on without me. The fact that he had a secret made Alfie feel important and on level terms with Fred.

He looked up at Tansy in Joe's arms and then rolled over and over at Joe's feet. The man laughed as Alfie got up and set off at a steady trot towards his own station.

'I'll plant some catmint for you,' Joe called after him.

Alfie glanced back. 'Miaow!' he cried. Good – I'll be back!

# 3

# Hack's Secret

Alfie slowed down before entering the station. He could hear Fred shouting and caught sight of Hack slouching about the platform, while the painters' brushes went swish, swish, swish across the wooden platform seats.

He sat down undecided. Should he turn back? No! The railway cat must be on duty. Warily he walked into the station. 'Miaow!' he greeted waiting passengers. I'm back.

'Hello!' said one man. 'Mind they don't paint you by mistake.'

'Miaow!' said Alfie. That's what I'm afraid of!

Fred bore down on him. 'I've been searching everywhere for you,' he cried reproachfully. 'I'm going to give you a good grooming . . .'

This was too much for Alfie. He started to run.

'Disobedient cat – come back!' yelled Fred, as he stood with arms akimbo and watched the railway cat weave his way between the passengers' legs. Alfie swerved to avoid Hack, but the leading railman moved quickly.

'Got you!' he shouted as he swooped and grabbed him by the tail.

'Mia . . ow . . . ow . . . .!' screeched Alfie as he struggled and scratched.

'Oh, no, you don't – not this time – you lazy, good-for-nothing animal,' roared Hack as he shook Alfie. 'Do you know, I actually saw a rat – a *rat*, do you hear? – on No. 1 platform this morning. Where's your sense of responsibility, your loyalty to the railway, your . . . ?'

But Alfie had heard enough. With a mighty struggle he freed himself and jumped down on to the platform with a thud. Where could he take refuge? In this confusion he barged into a ladder and nearly toppled a painter.

'Watch where you're going!' shouted the man, while Hack could be heard calling, 'Catch him – catch him!'

Looking round wildly for an escape route, Alfie saw the booking office door ajar. He streaked in and crouched underneath Brown's high stool. Brown appeared to be the only calm member of staff. He looked down.

'Hello, Alfie,' he said. 'Trying to avoid the turmoil? Don't blame you. Fred's secret is getting on everybody's nerves.'

'Miaow!' agreed Alfie quietly. But I've got a secret too.

Playfully, Brown dangled a piece of string over Alfie's nose. Alfie took a couple of swipes at it and missed.

The door was flung wide open. In came Hack. 'Seen anything of that cat?' he asked. 'Fred wants him.'

'Really?' said Brown innocently. 'Try the car park. Alfie usually patrols there once or twice a day.' Brown glanced through the open door and noticed painters moving ladders.

'Painters finished already?' he asked.

'No, worse luck,' said Hack. 'Fred's ordered them to go down the line to the old wayside

32

station and slap paint on the front of the waiting room – front only he told them. They're to ignore the back.' Hack shook his head. 'Don't know what's come over Fred since he started on this secret lark.'

Alfie flattened his ears in horror. The painters might discover Joe, and Tansy, and the secret garden – and it wouldn't be a secret any longer. He waited impatiently for Hack to go.

But the man lazed against the door. 'You'd think Fred was expecting a visit from royalty the way he's going on,' he said, with a sneer.

'Heavens, no!' laughed Brown. 'We'd have been advised of such an important event months, even years, ahead.'

'Well, it must be the General Manager, at least,' said Hack.

Alfie moved uneasily under the stool. Time was passing. The painters might already be on their way.

Fred could be heard calling, 'Hack! Hack! Bother the man. Where is he?'

Hack left hurriedly. Alfie crawled from

under the stool and made for the door. Brown turned round. 'Hey, there, Alfie, where are you off to now?'

'Miaow!' cried Alfie, as his tail disappeared round the door. On secret business – and quickly.

Rarely had Alfie's legs covered the distance to the disused station at such speed. Would he be in time to warn Joe before the painters arrived? He found Joe on his knees in the secret garden, while Tansy slept in an old basket nearby. Alfie immediately launched himself on to Joe's back.

'Hey!' cried Joe, taken by surprise. 'Oh, it's only you – what a relief. Back so soon? What's the matter this time?' He laughed as he tried to rise from his knees.

But Alfie clung on to his shoulders and pinned him down. On the alert, the railway cat stiffened suddenly. Joe stayed still and listened, as sounds of a vehicle being driven slowly down the narrow rutted overgrown lane leading to the back of the station could be heard.

'Help!' muttered Joe. 'We shall have to

skedaddle!' Hastily Alfie jumped down and Joe threw garden tools into the bushes, picked up Tansy, basket and all, said, 'Thank you,' to Alfie before disappearing into his secret hiding place in a tangle of bushes in a corner.

Alfie ran round to the front of the station and sat down on the platform. He didn't know what he would do in an emergency, but he was determined to stay around until the danger had passed.

Two painters came on to the platform carrying ladders, paint and brushes. Much to Alfie's surprise Hack followed, holding a long-handled broom and shovel. He stopped in his tracks when he saw Alfie.

'What! *You* here?' was his ungracious greeting. 'Don't I see far too much of you at our own station? Fred's looking everywhere for you. Be off!'

Alfie refused to budge. He spat and hissed as Hack advanced brandishing his broom.

'Leave him alone, Hack!' shouted one of the painters. 'The railway cat's as much right here

as anyone. You're always at him.'

Grumbling, Hack started to brush the platform, while the painters set up ladders and
began to paint. Hack swept the dust and rubble
into a large mound. Then he looked round to

make sure the painters had their backs to him. He was just about to tip the rubbish on to the lines when one of the men turned round.

'Hi! Caught you, Hack!' he cried. 'Stop that dirty habit, or we'll report you.'

'Miaow!' added Alfie, loudly. He often does it that way.

Looking more disgruntled than ever, Hack began to use brush and shovel in the proper manner. When he had finished he lolled about, hands in pockets, looking about him. Suddenly he walked to the edge of the platform and with his back to the track gazed intently at the small waiting room.

Alfie watched him all the time. Why was the man so interested in the place?

Then Hack walked round to the back of the station. Nervously, Alfie followed. Was Hack going to explore the garden? But Hack stood back and surveyed the rear of the building. Then he turned and stared at the tangled garden. His eyes glinted. Alfie moved nearer.

'Mmmm . . .' said Hack out loud. 'Why

didn't I think of it before? Marvellous idea. Just large enough and a nice bit of garden. Put it in the wife's name. Make her happy to have a welcome bit of extra money.'

He noticed Alfie. 'Why are you following me round, nuisance?' he said, glaring at the railway cat. 'I'm not telling anyone yet – least of all you – what's in my mind. It's a secret.'

'Miaow!' growled Alfie. Glad to hear your mind's not entirely empty. Don't like the sound of your secret, but I've got a very important secret of my own to think about. Alfie followed Hack to the front of the station, where the men had finished painting.

'Looks almost as clean as my platform,' joked Hack.

*My* platform – what a cheek, thought Alfie. You'd think the man owned the place.

'Want a lift, Alfie?' asked a painter.

'Miaow!' said Alfie. No, thank you. I've got my own affairs to attend to. He turned tail and shot off round to the back of the station and into the undergrowth.

39

'Always contrary, that cat,' he heard Hack say. 'If it wasn't for Fred spoiling him, I'd train him, I'd . . .'

Alfie hissed. And I'd teach you better manners if only I had the chance!

He waited until the van had been driven off, then he pushed his way into the secret garden. 'Miaow!' he called.

Cautiously, Joe came out of hiding. 'Gone, have they?' he whispered as he put his head on one side and listened. 'I'll have to be more on my guard in future.' He smiled at Alfie. 'I heard them talking and I've learned your name – *Alfie!*'

Alfie stretched out his front paws and scratched furiously at the grass before rolling over on to his back. Joe bent down and pulled his ears. 'Come on, Alfie, show me what these intruders have been up to.'

Alfie led the way to the front of the station and Joe gazed in surprise at the newly-painted building. 'Why do the front only? To impress someone passing by train? Odd – very odd.'

'Miaow!' agreed Alfie. That's just what I think.

Leaving Joe to puzzle over the matter Alfie set off homewards, thankful that all was well with Joe and Tansy – so far . . . Also, he was very hungry.

# 4

# In the Coal Bunker

Alfie was on duty bright and early next morning. The station staff and then the painters soon followed.

'Good start, lads,' said Fred. 'At this rate we'll get everything ready in record time for tomorrow morning.'

'That means *you* keeping out of the way, Alfie,' said Hack rudely.

'Miaow!' said Alfie. And that means *you* getting a move on for once.

The early morning commuters started arriving and as no one else paid them any attention, Alfie greeted each one individually. They talked to him.

'I expect you'll be relieved when things return to normal, Alfie?'

'They've all gone mad – this station will never be the same again.'

'Think I'll take out a bus season ticket instead of a rail ticket.'

'Miaow!' said Alfie. Please don't do that!

Fred came along holding out a length of blue satin ribbon. 'I'm going to tie this round Alfie's neck tomorrow,' he announced.

'Huh! Bells on his toes next!' muttered Hack, who was standing nearby.

Fred ignored him. 'Alfie must look handsome for the children's sake,' he said.

'What children?' asked Hack.

'Ah . . .' said Fred mysteriously.

There and then Alfie decided that no one, not even Fred, was going to make him a laughing stock. Blue ribbon, indeed! Fred must be crazy. Alfie stayed around all day and from a safe distance watched the men at work and listened to Fred's frequent outbursts.

'Give this door knob a polish – oil this creaking gate – put some bleach in the water when you swill down the platforms.' Fred went on and on and on.

But, late in the evening, Fred couldn't think

of anything more which required attention. Thankfully the painters departed. Fred looked round the station. 'Don't think anyone, even Her Hi . . er . . er . . even anyone could find fault with this station,' he said with pride. He went home leaving Hack in charge of the station for the rest of the evening.

Alfie was resting on a platform seat when Hack crept up on him unawares. 'Ribbon round your neck now?' he said sarcastically. 'Always wanting to be in the limelight, always needing attention, that's you.'

Alfie opened one eye and looked up at him. Hack went on, 'Well, it wouldn't hurt anyone if you were missing tomorrow morning, would it? Fred would be worried, but it would serve him right for keeping everything a secret.'

Suddenly Hack swooped, grabbed Alfie and carried him off to the rear of the station.

'Miaow! Miaow! Mia . . ow . . . ow . . . .' howled Alfie at the top of his voice. Help! Help! Help! But the station was quiet and deserted. He struggled as Hack, clutching him firmly

round the middle, opened the heavy lid of an old coal bunker and thrust the railway cat into the depths.

'It's only for tonight and tomorrow morning, so make the best of it,' said Hack as he closed the lid.

'Miaow!' cried Alfie. It's cold, dark and dirty in here. Let me out! Let me out! But all he heard was the sound of Hack's retreating footsteps.

Alfie knew the yard was rarely used at night, so in all probability no one would hear him even if he howled his head off. He settled down carefully trying not to disturb the coal dust, but without success. He could feel the black stuff settling all over him.

After what seemed ages – in fact the nearby church had only struck the hour twice – he heard someone approaching. The lid was raised and moonlight streamed into the bunker.

Joyfully, Alfie prepared to leap out, but a hand restrained him and Hack said, 'I've brought your supper before I sign off duty.' Still holding on to Alfie, he placed a dish on the floor of the bunker.

Alfie glanced in disgust at pieces of minced beef floating in milk. Hack couldn't even take the trouble to use separate dishes! Slovenly, that's what he is, thought Alfie. Tensing himself, he tried to spring out but Hack's grip was too firm.

'Oh, keep still, you stupid cat,' he scolded. 'It's only a joke really. Just to get even with Fred. Eat your supper and be thankful.' He waited. But Alfie couldn't bear the thought of food and refused to eat or drink.

'Turn your nose up at good food, do you?' said Hack. 'All right. I'll take it away.' He reached down, took out the dish and placed it on the ground outside the bunker. He hesitated before shutting the lid and departing, muttering to himself, 'Overfed cat . . .'

Only a joke, thought Alfie? Despicable, that's what he is. Wait until I get out. I'll pay him back somehow. When he had calmed down, he resigned himself to spending the night in such a confined dreary place. As he curled up he felt the gritty coal dust settle into his eyes, his ears and his fur. He shuddered in the darkness. Never had he felt so dirty.

He lay still and quiet as the night dragged on. Then, just after the clock had chimed three, he heard footsteps. Very excited, he was about to start a loud complaining when a thought struck him.

What if the prowler was a criminal, who wouldn't welcome being disturbed by a cat? Or perhaps Hack had relented and had returned to release him? In either case, better wait.

Then, without warning, the lid of the bunker was flung open, a torch shone right into his eyes and a voice he recognised cried, 'Why – it's Alfie! What on earth are you doing down there? Out you come.' In one bound Alfie escaped from his prison.

Joe looked at him in dismay. 'Tut-tut . . . what a sorry sight you are,' he said. 'But, never mind, I'll soon clean you up.'

As he closed the lid he noticed the dish on the

ground. 'Food!' he exclaimed. 'Just what I've been searching for. Tansy needs nourishing food to help her recover from her ordeal in the tunnel. I'm sure you won't mind sharing this with her, Alfie?'

'Miaow!' cried Alfie, rubbing against Joe's legs. *She can have the lot, and welcome!*

Carefully carrying the dish, Joe led the way out of the station. 'We'll have to take the country lane back to the wayside station,' he told Alfie. 'It's far too dangerous for me to use the embankment. I might be seen and taken into custody for trespassing – and then what would happen to Tansy?'

After his experience in the coal bunker Alfie thoroughly enjoyed walking in the moonlight with Joe. Once he heard something scuttling in the hedgerow and darted towards the sound. Flat on his stomach he waited on the alert, but nothing moved. After a time he decided there were more important matters to be dealt with and hastened after Joe.

Joe looked down at him and smiled.

'Thought you'd deserted me,' he said.

'Miaow!' said Alfie. Never.

'I'd like to know who shut you up in that ghastly bunker,' Joe said indignantly. 'I'd give him what-for!'

'Miaow!' said Alfie again. It's about time somebody put Hack in his place.

They turned down the narrow lane leading to the back of the old station. When they reached the secret garden Joe put the dish on the ground and went to fetch Tansy from the hide-out. When they returned Joe put the kitten down in front of the dish and Alfie watched as she lapped a little milk and nibbled some meat.

'Little and often, that's the menu for a young kitten,' said Joe as he bent to pick Tansy up. 'Now we're going inside the waiting room for a good sleep,' he said. 'Camp-bed's ready. Coming, Alfie?'

'Miaow!' said Alfie. Yes, please.

Then, 'Miaow!' No, thank you. On second thoughts I'm far too dirty to come inside. I'll have a go at cleaning myself.

Joe waited. 'No? Oh, all right,' he said. 'See you in an hour or so. I'll have to do some very early morning gardening if I am to make more money.' Shining the torch he carried Tansy into the waiting room and closed the door.

Alfie waited until the light went out before he started on himself. It was hard work. His fur was so full of coal dust that no amount of licking made much difference.

Goodness, he thought! This is going to take the rest of the night. Soon the licking became slower and slower and eventually Alfie gave up altogether. He lay down thinking how good it was to relax in the fresh air after being shut up in that horrible coal bunker.

He had lost all interest in Fred's secret. As for Hack's secret – well, he didn't want to know anything about *that*. He, Alfie, had got his own special secret, which for Joe's sake, no one must ever discover.

Alfie decided he would never, never return to his own station – at least not for a long, long time. He'd definitely stay away until the place

was overrun with rats and mice. Then everyone, even Hack, would be overjoyed to see him.

In the meantime he was quite content to be
the old disused station's railway cat. He began
to feel hungry and as he dozed off he admitted to
himself that he would miss tomorrow's liver,
which Fred provided once a week.

But, never mind, his secret was more important than food, even if liver was his favourite
dish. Or was it? What about the Christmas
turkey, or a nice cod steak, or even a plump
pork sausage . . . ? Dreaming of food, he fell
fast asleep.

## 5

# Very Special Visitors

Alfie woke to find himself surrounded by a thin dawn mist. He got up when he heard a door opening. Joe came out of the waiting room.

'Good morning, my friend!' he said as he bent down and scratched the back of Alfie's head between the ears.

"Prrr . . rrr . . . rr . . . .' sang Alfie. I like that – do it again!

Playfully Joe ruffled his fur and a cloud of coal dust rose into the air. 'Phew! You do look a mess,' laughed Joe. 'But don't worry. First, digging – then, before I go off with my barrow-load of vegetables, I'll get busy on you with sponge, brush and comb. You'll look as good as new.'

'Tansy's still asleep,' Joe went on. 'I'll share the food between you later. Amuse yourself for a little while.'

'Miaow!' said Alfie. Certainly.

He went round to the front of the station and sat down on the platform. Soon a train passed on the Up line. The driver waved. Not long afterwards a freight train trundled through the station. The driver saluted. Very satisfactory, thought Alfie. He always enjoyed being recognised by his fellow railway workers.

Time passed and there was no sign of Joe or Tansy. Might as well have another go at cleaning myself while I'm waiting, decided Alfie. He hoped Joe wouldn't go on digging all morning as he was beginning to feel really hungry.

Alfie spread out the toes of his right forepaw intending to lick them clean, when he heard another train approaching from the London direction. With his tongue hanging out he watched the train, puzzled, for it was slowing down.

Good gracious – it's going to stop *here*, thought Alfie! How strange. It must be a ghost train. Or perhaps it had something to do with Fred's secret? Was it a special train? It didn't

look special. He waited fascinated as the two-coach diesel drew up at the platform.

A door opened and out stepped a boy and a girl, followed by a lady. A door further down the train burst open at the same time and an attendant rushed forward. 'Excuse me, ma'am,' he gasped. 'The driver has made a mistake. This is the wrong station. We are expected at the *next* one.' He beckoned to the children to get back into the train.

'But I want to stay and see over this little station,' cried the girl. 'It looks gorgeous.'

'Yes, just the kind of station we wanted to visit,' said the boy as he peered through a chink in the window-boards. 'There's a waiting room and a booking office!'

'And there's a CAT,' shouted the girl as she caught sight of Alfie. 'He's very dirty but he's got lovely greeny-yellow eyes and he looks friendly.'

The children rushed up to Alfie, who arched his back and purred a welcome as they stroked and petted him.

The attendant was very worried. 'Please, ma'am,' he said. 'We're already ten minutes late for our appointment.'

The lady looked at the children and smiled. 'They really are enjoying themselves, Thompson,' she said. 'We'll let them stay for just a few minutes.'

Without warning, Joe, carrying Tansy, appeared round a corner of the waiting room. He halted in astonishment when he saw the group on the platform. 'Good heavens – royalty – a princess!' he muttered as he turned to flee.

But the princess put up a hand and called out, 'Wait a minute, please.'

The children ran up to Joe. 'There's a kitten as well,' cried the girl. 'Poor little thing, it's injured.'

'Tansy will soon be well again,' Joe assured her. He was very embarrassed at being the centre of attention.

'Tansy – what a lovely name,' said the princess as she shook hands with Joe. 'We are

supposed to be at the next station on a very private visit,' she told him. 'The children are interested in railways and wanted to be shown round a station as other children are.'

While the children, and Alfie, rushed about examining everything, the princess talked to Joe, and when he had overcome his shyness, he told her about being out of work.

Thompson joined them. 'Please, ma'am,' he said again. 'We must be holding up other trains on the line.'

'Oh, dear, I am sorry,' she said. 'We'd better hurry. Come children –' But the children, and Alfie, had disappeared.

'They must have gone round to the back, ma'am,' said Joe.

'Well, we'd better go and find them, quickly,' said the princess.

At the rear of the waiting room, the princess gazed in surprise at the peeling paintwork and broken window. 'What one might call "putting a good front on it"!' she said with a twinkle in her eyes.

The children could not be seen, but shouts were heard and Joe said, 'I know where they are,' as he parted the bushes for the princess to go through.

They found the children, and Alfie, in the secret garden chasing about all over the place. Alfie stopped to dig his claws into the bark of a tree, pulling them in and out, in and out in his excitement.

'I'm sure this is the very best station in the whole world,' shouted the boy.

'And this is a *secret* garden!' added the girl.

'I can see that,' said the princess smiling. She turned to Joe. 'Is this your garden?'

Joe hung his head. 'Well, not really, ma'am,' he admitted. 'I use it – without permission – to grow vegetables for sale. It's my livelihood.' He hesitated. 'We – Tansy and me, that is – we'll have to go now I've been found out.'

The princess looked sympathetic. 'Well, we'll see . . .' she said as she glanced round. 'It's a very well-kept little garden. You're going to have a good healthy crop of vegetables.'

She turned to the children. 'No nonsense, now,' she said firmly. 'We really must be on our way.'

'Oh, no – *please*. We're enjoying ourselves,' they cried.

'Miaow!' cried Alfie. Me too!

Suddenly Alfie rushed into the bushes. Before the princess could stop them the children followed, pushing through shrubs which pricked them and tore their clothes. They came to Joe's hide-out in a corner and with shrieks of excitement they examined the camp-bed, the first aid box and Joe's bits and pieces, which were all he possessed in the world.

'We could hide here for weeks and weeks,' shouted the boy.

'For months and months,' echoed the girl.

'Prrr . . rrr . . . rrr . . . .' said Alfie. For ever perhaps!

But the princess was calling, 'Children, children – *we must be going*!'

And Joe shouted as he pushed his way through the bushes, 'I'll bring them back.'

Soon, laughing and shouting, the children returned to the waiting princess.

She put a hand to her lips when she saw them. 'Oh!' she exclaimed. '*Oh!* Look at your clothes – and your hair – and your faces and . . . Well, you'll have to come along as you are. There's no time left to clean you up. We've kept our hosts waiting long enough as it is.' Reluctantly the children followed her.

'Look after Tansy,' the princess called to Joe. She glanced at Alfie. 'And soap and water wouldn't come amiss on him.' She laughed. 'But it isn't every day we find a cat and a kitten – and a nice grown-up – in a secret garden.'

Joe, with Tansy, and Alfie followed the group back to the platform. As the princess led the way into the train she said, 'Here we go on our way to the real station.'

That's *my* station, thought Alfie proudly. He felt sorry he wouldn't be on duty to greet the royal party. Whatever would Fred say if he saw him covered in coal dust? But wasn't it part of

the railway cat's duties to be in attendance for special occasions? And wasn't this a very special occasion?

Alfie looked up at Joe, who nodded. The railway cat made up his mind. In one bound, just as the door was closing, he leapt into the train. Scampering down the gangway he jumped on to the seat occupied by the royal children, who immediately hugged him. Clouds of black dust covered all three.

The princess looked on in dismay. 'Oh, dear,' she said in a flurry. 'I'll have to try and do something about you.' She glanced out of the window. 'Oh, *dear*,' she said again, helplessly. 'The train's slowing down. There isn't time!'

'Miaow!' cried Alfie, very excited. True. There isn't time. We're nearly there and some people are in for a very big surprise . . .

# 6

## Good News

Everything looks very smart, thought Alfie, as the train drew into his station. His eyes widened when he saw Fred, Hack, Brown and the rest of the staff lined up each side of a strip of red carpet, which had been laid on the platform. A flower arrangement on a tall pedestal looked very decorative. Trust Fred to do the job properly!

The train stopped. Alfie leapt off the seat and was first at the door. It was opened from the outside and as the staff waited expectantly for the royal party to alight – out stepped a very dirty cat!

Fred cried, 'Oh, *no*!' before clapping a hand to his mouth, while Hack muttered, 'Blimey – trust Alfie!' The staff stared in disbelief at the unkempt railway cat and the two royal children, their faces and clothes smeared with coal dust.

With head held high and the tip of his tail waving, Alfie led the little procession along the carpet. When the princess stopped to speak to a member of staff, Alfie stopped. When she continued walking, Alfie did the same. Once he was compelled to sit down and have a really good scratch with his left hind leg. Black coal dust settled on the red carpet as he did so.

Fred hissed, 'Stop that, Alfie!'

'But what is he supposed to do when he itches?' asked the boy.

'Coal dust is such irritating stuff,' said the princess. 'I must apologise for my children's appearance today.'

The morning passed very quickly as Fred conducted the royal party on a tour of the station. Alfie went along as well, although twice Fred tried to wave him away and Hack said from the corner of his mouth, 'Disgusting behaviour!'

The children were very polite and interested in everything. When the visit came to an end and everybody had been thanked, the boy said,

'We like this station very much, but the little one up the line *is* rather special.'

'Yes – with Joe and the kitten and the secret garden,' added the girl.

'Joe? Kitten? Secret garden?' said Fred, puzzled. He turned to the princess. 'I don't understand what they mean, ma'am.'

So she told him about Joe and Tansy and the garden.

'Well, of all the cheek,' muttered Hack. 'A man making use of my . . .' He stopped and looked round furtively.

The children said an affectionate farewell to Alfie before they boarded the train for the homeward journey. 'He's the most intelligent cat we've ever met,' said the boy.

Alfie glanced sideways at Hack. Then he sat on the platform with paws together and tail neatly tucked in as the train departed, with the children and their mother waving from a window.

After all the excitement Alfie felt rather tired and was making his way towards the staff room, with the easy chair in mind, when Fred caught up with him.

'Oh, no, you don't, Alfie!' he cried. 'Not until I've cleaned you up – and how you need it.'

'He's an absolute disgrace to the railway, that cat,' said Hack. 'Dirty, unreliable and I'm sure it was his fault the royal party was late . . .'

'Oh, shut up, Hack!' cried Fred, exasperated. He picked Alfie up and took him along to a quiet corner of the platform. And there, for the first time in his life, Alfie actually *enjoyed* a very good wash and brush-up.

Afterwards Alfie had his first meal of the day – liver, his favourite food, which in spite of all the goings-on Fred had remembered to bring for him. Good old Fred. Alfie sighed with contentment.

Things settled down again after the royal visit. Of course, Alfie's secret was now common knowledge. Everyone knew about Joe but, so far, no one had ordered him off the old station.

'It's a matter for Headquarters to decide,'

said Fred, when anyone raised the question as to whether Joe should be told to leave or not. 'Joe is trespassing, but he's really a very honest, industrious person and you never know . . .'

But Alfie was worried. He often walked along the embankment to visit Joe and Tansy. Occasionally Fred went as well, taking with him a loaf of bread or some home-made cakes for Joe and liver or lights, or perhaps a cod's head, for the kitten.

To everyone's surprise Hack often went to the old station, where he would glance round in a secretive manner. He was always irritated when he met Alfie there.

'Can't have *you* lurking about here,' he would say.

'Miaow!' Alfie would hiss. What's it got to do with you where I am? You and your silly secret.

One day when Alfie arrived at the wayside station he found Fred and Hack talking to Joe. Hack was very annoyed when he saw Alfie.

'You here again – always poking your nose into other people's affairs,' he shouted. 'Wish

71

I'd locked you in that coal bunker for good.'

'What!' yelled Fred, red in the face. 'You mean to say *you* did that to Alfie? Our Alfie, the friendliest and most efficient cat we've ever had?'

Alfie rolled over and over gleefully.

'You scoundrel!' cried Joe, his eyes flashing. 'I'd like to shut you up in that coal bunker for a whole month without food or drink.'

'And it would give me great pleasure to send you down a coal mine for good,' added Fred. He glared at Hack, who went crimson, shuffled his feet and looked ashamed.

'It was only a joke really,' he murmured.

'Joke!' cried Fred and Joe in unison, while Alfie growled, 'Brrr . . brrr . . . brrr . . . .'

'What have you got against Alfie? Why shouldn't he come here as often as he likes?' said Fred. 'And if it comes to that, why do you haunt the place?'

'Yes, tell us that,' put in Joe. 'You're always prowling round, watching me.'

Hack glanced up and down the line, looked at

his watch and announced, 'Well, it's time for me to report for duty. I'll be off.' He started to walk away.

'Not before you've given us an answer,' said Fred, blocking his path.

'And a true one,' said Joe.

'Well, er . . . as a matter of fact,' began Hack. 'Er . . . well, it's no business of yours!'

'Oh, yes, it is,' said Fred firmly.

'But it's a secret,' shouted Hack.

'Let us into the secret then,' said Fred, as he stared hard at Hack.

'Oh, well, I suppose you'll all have to know sooner or later,' he said. 'I've made an offer to buy this little station for my wife. She intends making it into a holiday cottage and renting it to people in the summer to make some extra money for us.'

Alfie couldn't believe his ears. A holiday cottage? What about Joe and the garden – and Tansy? Very worried, he looked up at Fred, who for the moment was dumbstruck, while Joe was filled with dismay. Fred was the first to pull himself together. He patted Joe on the shoulder.

'Don't worry, Joe,' he said. 'His offer hasn't been accepted yet.'

'Oh, but I'm sure it's in the bag,' boasted Hack. 'I expect an acceptance of my offer by post tomorrow morning.'

And next morning's post did bring a reply for Hack – but it wasn't what he had hoped for. He brought the letter to show Fred. 'They won't let me buy the old station,' he raged.

Fred said nothing.

'And it's that cat's fault – making up to royalty as he did,' Hack went on.

'It's got nothing to do with Alfie,' said Fred. 'Come on, Hack, trains won't wait while we stand here talking.'

Next day Joe came along to Alfie's station. He also had received a letter, which he handed to Fred to read. The smile on Fred's face broadened as his eyes scanned the page.

'Why, Joe, this is good news,' he cried. 'You're to be a tenant of the old station. Hear that, Alfie? And the building is to be modernised and made into a small dwelling.'

'Prrr . . rrrr . . . rrrr . . . .' said Alfie. Best bit of news I've ever heard.

Hack came along. 'Listen to this, Hack,' said Fred. He read the letter out loud.

'Oh!' said Hack when Fred had finished. He looked down at the platform and shuffled his feet. Then he drew himself up, went across and shook hands with Joe. 'Congratulations, Joe,' he said. 'I'm sure you need the station and garden more than I do.'

'Miaow!' cried Alfie, astonished. Well, I never! But that's the spirit. One day I might *possibly* understand Hack.

Alfie jumped up at Joe, then with the tip of his tail waving, raced along the platform, leapt on and off seats, trucks and mail bags, before running over the bridge and back again to the group.

'Well done, Alfie,' laughed Fred. 'Now back to work everyone.'

Alfie kept a watchful eye on developments at

Joe's station. Very soon the waiting room became a living room, the ticket office a bedroom, and a small bathroom was built on at the back.

In between gardening and selling the produce, Joe painted the back of the building, weeded between the platform slabs, mended the fence and gate, put a new brass knocker on the front door and dug up the uncultivated part of the garden. Eventually everything was completed and the wayside station was declared open for the sale of fruit and vegetables.

Joe worked harder than ever. Alfie wished he could urge all passengers to go along and buy his fruit and vegetables. He need not have worried, for Fred – and to Alfie's surprise Hack also – distributed leaflets to passengers and villagers giving information about Joe's new nursery garden.

And everyone was happy – everyone that is, except Hack, who often looked very *unhappy*. Alfie felt sorry about this for he didn't like anyone to be miserable.

Could anything be done to help Hack?

# The Old Railway Carriage

Day by day Alfie watched Hack as the man shuffled along the platforms and answered passengers' questions in a surly manner. Whatever *could* one do to help such a miserable man, thought Alfie? One day he overheard Fred taking Hack to task about his shortcomings.

'The fact is, I'm worn out,' said Hack. 'The wife keeps on and on and on about missing the chance to buy the little station – as though it was my fault.' He glared at Alfie. 'That cat has a lot to answer for.'

'Nonsense!' said Fred shortly. 'I'm sorry you are worried but passengers have been complaining about your manners and I won't have that while I'm in charge of the station.'

Stern words from Fred, thought Alfie.

Hack was silent as he looked down at the

floor. 'Well, I'll just have to try harder to be pleasant,' he said at last.

One day Alfie decided to go for a walk through the surrounding fields, as a change from his station work. He gambolled about in the long grass enjoying the spring sunshine and chasing everything that moved. At the end of a small field he came across a shed. At least, at first glance, it looked like a shed, but on closer inspection it turned out to be an old railway carriage.

Alfie walked round the carriage until he came to a door. He pushed it open and entered the carriage. The door closed behind him. He looked round with interest. The place was bare, but there was evidence that the farmer had recently used the carriage as a large chicken coop. Feathers lay about the floor.

Alfie nosed round. No mice. What a pity. Nothing left for them to nibble now the chicken feed had disappeared, he supposed. Rays from the setting sun shone through the grimy window panes. Time to go, he thought. He made for the door, forgetting it had closed behind him. There was no other exit.

Trapped again! Was it his lot in life to be shut up in undesirable places, thought Alfie? All he could do was sit down on the dusty floor and wait patiently in the hope that someone would come along and let him out.

He listened to birds singing, and to the pitter-patter of their feet on the carriage roof. Small creatures scuttled round and under the carriage. By the end of the second day of his captivity he was sure he wouldn't be able to last much longer without food and drink. Never had he felt so frustrated.

Next morning, however, he heard sounds in the distance. He pricked up his ears. The sounds came nearer. Then Alfie got up and rushed to the door excitedly, for he recognised Hack's voice calling.

'Digby! Heel, I say – come back!'

'Woof! Woof! Woof!' barked a dog.

Alfie guessed that Hack was taking his dog, Digby, for a walk through the fields and that

Digby had sensed his, Alfie's, presence in the carriage. Alfie's miaowing and banging against the door became more frenzied. He couldn't bear the thought of Hack catching Digby and leading him away without coming into the carriage. But, to his relief, Alfie heard Digby barking as he jumped up the door.

'Woof! Woof! Woof!' howled Digby.

'Miaow! Miaow! Miaow!' cried Alfie.

'Caught you!' cried Hack and Alfie heard the man fastening the lead on to Digby's collar. 'I'll tie you to this hook for a time – teach you to obey orders.'

Alfie fell back as the door opened. Hack entered and closed the door behind him. He started in surprise when he saw Alfie. 'Well, well, Alfie, you're a right one for getting locked in, aren't you?' he said as he gave Alfie a friendly pat. 'You must have been here for two or three days. Hungry, I expect? Fred's been out the last two nights looking for you.'

Hands in pockets, Hack gazed round the carriage. 'Hmmm . . . it's a more cheerful place than the coal bunker,' he said. 'But that was only for a few hours.'

'Miaow!' wailed Alfie. I've forgotten about the coal bunker, but let me out, please. I *am* hungry!

Hack hadn't finished his inspection. Slowly he paced the length and breadth of the carriage. Then he stood right in the middle and stared ahead, deep in thought. Suddenly he snapped his fingers and cried, 'The very thing! Back to the station, Alfie, I've got some business to do.' He flung the door wide open.

Alfie didn't wait for a skirmish with Digby. Off he sped back to the station and Fred.

Fred was so pleased to see him that he forgot to scold. Instead he rushed into the staff room and prepared Alfie's first meal for three days – a dish of fish and a saucer of cream. Cream! Almost worth the discomfort of being locked up, thought Alfie, as he started on his meal.

Soon Hack arrived. The man was panting with the effort of controlling Digby on the lead. Digby surged forward when he saw Alfie but

Hack pulled him back and ordered him to sit down.

Fred looked up surprised. 'Hello!' he said. 'What's brought you here before duty time?'

Hack could hardly get the words out. 'Fo . . . found Alfie in that old carriage by the stream in Farmer Lunt's field,' he gasped. 'Had a . . . a . . . a brilliant idea. With a few alterations that old carriage could be made into an ideal holiday cottage – in open country, not far from the station.'

Hack sighed. 'If only Lunt would let me buy it.'

'Well . . . there's a chance he might,' said Fred thoughtfully. 'I heard a few weeks ago that he was prepared to sell the carriage, and a patch of ground, if a suitable offer came along.'

'Really?' shouted Hack, his eyes shining.

Fred nodded. 'But don't forget,' he said, 'you might never have known about the carriage if Alfie hadn't been shut in and if Digby hadn't led you to him.' Fred winked at Alfie. 'Excellent cat, our Alfie!'

84

'Er . . . yes . . . er, yes, he is,' said Hack, with a lop-sided grin at Alfie. 'Sometimes!' he added. He and Digby set off homewords.

And in due time the old railway carriage became a holiday cottage. Hack, assisted at times by Fred and Joe – and hindered by Alfie getting in the way – worked hard on the carriage making it comfortable for visitors. But it would never, never look as attractive as Joe's wayside station, Alfie decided.

Hack was a changed man. When on duty he was helpful and courteous to passengers, and occasionally he stopped to stroke Alfie and have a word with him.

'Wonders will never cease!' marvelled Fred.

Alfie was pleased, but he wasn't going to accept too much attention from Hack. He didn't think the man would ever really like cats. However, for the time being, Alfie was content to be friends.

The station settled down into its ordinary routine until one day Fred made an announcement. 'The royal train – the *real* royal train –

will be passing through the station next Tuesday.' He grinned at Alfie. 'I understand some of the royal children will be on board. Think you'll get a wave, Alfie?'

'Miaow!' cried Alfie. Sure I will.

When Tuesday came, Alfie was in a dilemma. Should he stay at his own station, or should he go along to Joe's wayside station to be with his two friends when the royal train went past?

He decided that Fred could manage without him, so off he went along the now familiar route. Tansy, completely recovered, waited quietly beside Joe as Alfie, unable to control his excitement, dashed up and down the platform and round and round the garden.

'Calm down!' laughed Joe.

And soon, 'Here it comes!' he shouted as he stood to attention, white handkerchief at the ready to wave.

The bright, gleaming royal train (not a two-coach diesel this time) slackened speed as it approached the wayside station. Was it going to stop here, thought Alfie? The train didn't halt

but it slowed down so that two children – two clean and tidy children – could lean out of a window and wave vigorously at the man, cat and kitten on the platform.

Joe waved back, Tansy rolled over on to her side while Alfie rushed to the end of the platform alongside the train as it gathered speed. Joe called him back in case, in his enthusiasm, the railway cat followed the royal train into the tunnel!

Alfie stayed for a time and watched Joe at work. Customers now came from far and near to buy his fruit and vegetables, which were the best Alfie had ever seen. He thought he had never seen anyone work as hard as Joe.

Although Joe was such a busy man, he never forgot to grow plenty of catmint for his friend Alfie, the railway cat. And Alfie often visited the wayside station to play with Tansy in the garden, which was no longer a secret garden, but one which had received *royal* approval –

*Other Young Puffins by Phyllis Arkle*

### THE RAILWAY CAT
and
### THE RAILWAY CAT AND DIGBY

More stories about Alfie and his sworn enemy Hack the porter, in which Alfie tries to win over Hack by various means, often with hilarious results.

### MAGIC AT MIDNIGHT

Wild Duck discovers that anything can move while the clock is striking midnight, so he enjoys a new life with friends from the other Inn signs, The Lion and the Fiddle, the Unicorn and the Mermaid.

### MAGIC IN THE AIR

At night, and when it's misty, the weathervane witch (who keeps dropping her broomstick), the weathercock and the weatherdragon all come to life.

## THE VILLAGE DINOSAUR

Dino was a real dinosaur and Jed was thrilled, but the village said it was too big and a nuisance, until it proved it could help in some important ways.

## TWO VILLAGE DINOSAURS

Two dinosaurs spell double trouble as Dino and Sauro trample their amiable way through the village.

*Some other Young Puffins*

## THE BUREAUCRATS
### *Richard Adams*

Two kittens who think themselves the most important members of a large household soon learn otherwise, with highly entertaining consequences.

## RAGDOLLY ANNA'S CIRCUS
### *Jean Kenward*

Made only from a morsel of this and a tatter of that Ragdolly Anna is a very special doll, whose adventures are based on the television series.

## ON THE NIGHT WATCH
### *Hannah Cole*

A group of children and their parents occupy their tiny school in an effort to prevent its closure.

## ONE NIL

### Tony Bradman

Dave Brown is mad about football, and when he learns that the England squad are to train at the local City ground he thinks up a brilliant plan to overcome his parents' objections and gets to the ground to see them. A very amusing story.

## THE GHOST AT No. 13

### Gyles Brandreth

Hamlet Brown's sister, Susan, is just too perfect. Everything she does is praised and Hamlet is in despair – until the ghost comes to stay for a holiday and helps him to find an exciting idea for his school project.

## ZOZU THE ROBOT

### Diana Carter

Rufus and Sarah find a tiny frightened little robot and his space capsule in their garden.

## RADIO ALERT
## RADIO DETECTIVE

*John Escott*

Two exciting stories centred around a local radio station, Roundbay Radio. There's a mystery in each book which the children involved help to solve brilliantly.

## FIONA FINDS HER TONGUE

*Diana Hendry*

At Home Fiona is a chatterbox but whenever she goes out she just won't say a word. How she overcomes her shyness and 'finds her tongue' is told in this charming story.

## THE THREE AND MANY WISHES
## OF JASON REID

*Hazel Hutchins*

Jason is eleven and a very good thinker so when he is granted three wishes he is very wary indeed. After all, he knows the tangles that happen in fairy stories!